MOUSEKIN'S FROSTY FRIEND

To Florrie, Doris and Chris

MOUSEKIN'S FROSTY FRIEND

STORY AND PICTURES BY
EDNA MILLER

SIMON AND SCHUSTER BOOKS FOR YOUNG READERS

Published by Simon & Schuster Inc.
New York • London • Toronto • Sydney • Tokyo • Singapore

SIMON AND SCHUSTER
BOOKS FOR YOUNG READERS
Simon & Schuster Building
Rockefeller Center
1230 Avenue of the Americas
New York, New York 10020

SIMON AND SCHUSTER BOOKS FOR YOUNG READERS
is a trademark of Simon & Schuster Inc.

Manufactured in the United States of America

10 9 8 7 6 5 4 3 2 1

Library of Congress Cataloging-in-Publication Data
Miller, Edna, 1920-   Mousekin's frosty friend / Edna Miller.
p.   cm.   Summary: Among many other animal tracks in the snow,
Mousekin finds a set of unfamiliar and puzzling tracks, the origin of which
is eventually revealed.   1. Mice—Juvenile fiction.   [1. Mice—Fiction.
2. Animal tracks—Fiction.]   I. Title.   PZ10.3.M5817Ma1
1990   [Fic]—dc20   89-29892   ISBN 0-671-70445-1

Snowflakes fell softly and silently all day,
and now they blanketed the forest floor.
A full moon rose in a cloudless sky,
casting long shadows on the snow.
The bright moonlight awakened Mousekin
as it shone into his snug little nest
high up in a long-needled pine.

The white-footed mouse peered outside
with his bright, shoe-button eyes,
and he listened for danger with his large ears —
for owls and hawks and other creatures
that hunt mice on a wintry night.

When Mousekin was certain nothing stirred
but the wind in the long-needled pine,
he scampered between the branches
to search for pinecone seeds.

While he nibbled and gnawed,
he watched below as friendly creatures
passed his way and left their tracks
in the new-fallen snow.

A cottontail rabbit hopped from the brush
to feed on a stand of bare twigs.

A raccoon ambled through the woods
to hunt for food in the night.

A squirrel, tricked by moonlight
bright as day, scampered across the snow
to find an acorn buried long ago.

Mousekin hopped to a lower branch
on the far side of the tree,
and just as he reached for a pinecone
there, he looked below to see...

a giant of snow standing stark and still
in a grove of small evergreen trees.
It had black walnut eyes, a pinecone nose,
and a crooked twig for its mouth.
It wore a red woolen cap on its head.

Around the towering figure
were tracings in the snow.
Long, deep grooves ran side by side
with footprints all about.
No creature Mousekin knew
could leave such tracks behind.
Mousekin crouched; he watched and
waited; but the stranger never moved.
When he was certain he had nothing
to fear, he hurried down the tree
to where the snowman stood.

He circled about the snowy form.
With hops and jumps he reached the top
to the soft, woolen cap on its head.

As Mousekin was pulling some wool from
the cap to line his nest in the tree,
he heard a chickadee's early call.
There were stores of food to be found
in the woods before the break of day.

The little mouse jumped to the ground below
and ran through the evergreen grove.
There were tracks of many creatures now
that crisscrossed on the snow.
A hungry fox saw the paw prints, too!
He followed the ones that Mousekin made.

As Mousekin uncovered his find of food
at the base of a hickory tree,
the chickadee gave a warning call.
Mousekin dove for cover.
He tunneled back to the evergreen trees
and his home in the long-needled pine.

The fox followed the shifting snow
as the little mouse made his way below.
When Mousekin dared to peek above,
he saw the snowman there. With a leap
and a bound, he reached its top,
and hid in the red woolen cap.

The fox caught sight
of the snowman, too!
He stopped in his tracks,
and with a "yap!"
he turned and raced away.

When Mousekin was certain the fox
had gone, he left his soft, warm perch
and hurried to other stores of food
before the sun came up.

He raced between a
hollow log and his nest
in the long-needled pine.
He carried nuts and seeds
he'd hidden long before
the snow.

A screech owl hunted white-footed
mice to fill her empty nest.
When she spied Mousekin
on a branch of the tree,
she swooped to snatch her prey.

Mousekin's sharp ears heard
the click of her bill, and he
jumped to the ground below.
He tunneled to where the
snowman stood. Then, leaping
to the top once more, he dove
beneath its cap.

The hungry owl flew
about the tree when
Mousekin disappeared.
She hunted in the
evergreen grove 'til she
spied the staring figure of
snow with the red woolen
cap on its head. When
she heard the giant
squeak, she whirled about
in terror and flew off into
the woods.

When Mousekin dared to look outside,
he saw the first pale light of dawn
had colored the snow-filled forest.
He hurried back to his nest in the pine
to sleep the day away.

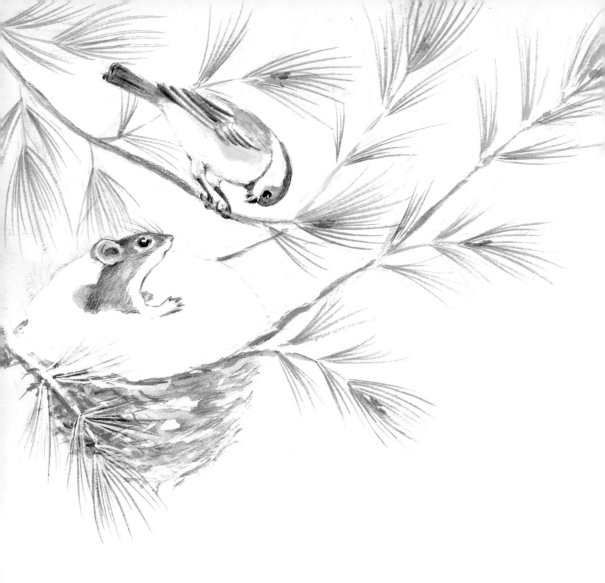

Mousekin slept soundly and never stirred
'til the chickadee called at dusk...
"Chick-a-dee-dee-dee...Come see! Come see!
There's a treat for all on the evergreen tree!"

When Mousekin hopped outside
his nest and looked toward the
evergreen grove, he saw his
frosty friend still there, but
one small tree nearby was gone.

The other tree was decked with food:
Strings of popcorn, apple slices,
peanuts, and cranberry strands
hung from every branch.
Cake crumbs and sunflower seeds
were strewn beneath the tree.

There were animal tracks
from all directions as woodland
creatures came to feed.
Mousekin raced down
to join the feast. He didn't
see the two long grooves
with footprints all about
that wove their way
between the trees and
out into a clearing.